Growing Vegetable Soup

Written and illustrated by Lois Ehlert

Harcourt, Inc.

San Diego   New York   London

DEDICATED TO MY FELLOW GARDENERS:
GLADYS, HARRY, JOHN, AND JAN

Library of Congress Cataloging-in-Publication Data
Ehlert, Lois.
Growing vegetable soup.
Summary: A father and child grow vegetables and then
make them into a soup.
[1. Vegetable gardening—Fiction.   2. Soups—Fiction.]
I. Title.
PZ7.E44Gr   1987   [E]   86-22812
ISBN 0-15-232575-1
ISBN 0-15-232580-8 pb
ISBN 0-15-232581-6 oversize pb

V U T S R Q P O

Printed in Singapore

Dad says we are going to grow vegetable soup.

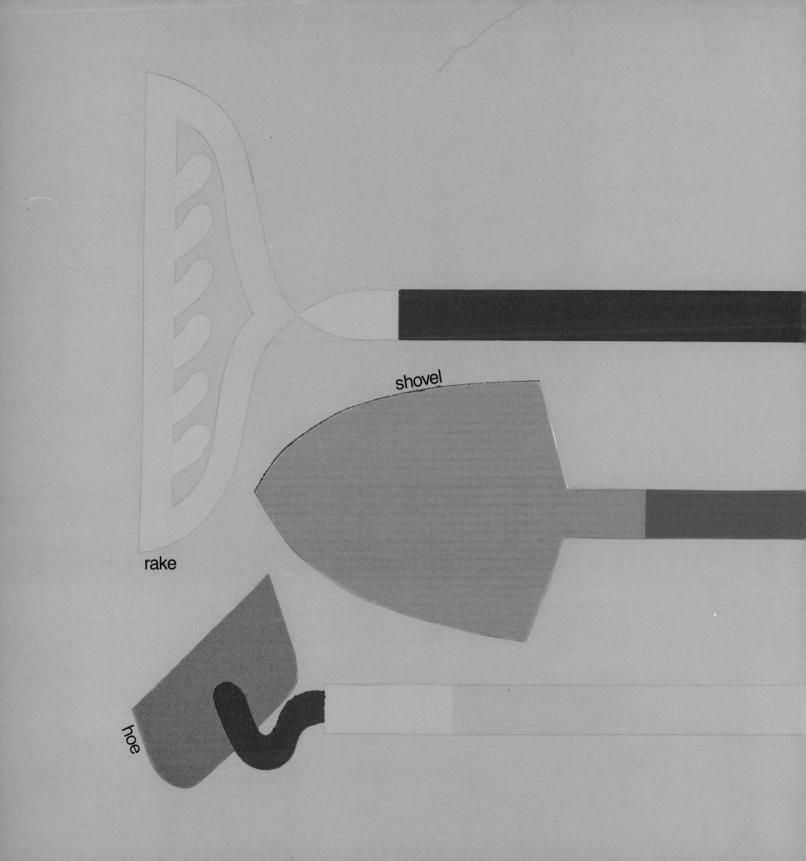

rake

shovel

hoe

We're ready to work,

and our tools are

ready, too.

We are planting

seed package

soil

hole

the seeds,

garden glove

green bean
seed

pea
seed

corn
seed

zucchini squash
seed

carrot
seeds

and all the sprouts,

broccoli

TOMATO

potato eyes

trowel

PEPPER

CABBAGE

set onions

peat moss pot

and giving them water,

water

PEPPER

ZUCCHINI SQUASH

PEA

ONION

BROCCOLI

CORN

and waiting for warm sun to make them grow,

and grow,

soil

ZUCCHINI SQUASH

ONION

POTATO

PEA

CARROT

CORN

weed

and grow into plants.

net

stake

PEA

soil

squash
bud

ZUCCHINI SQUASH

squash
blossom

We watch

worm

BROCCOLI

over them and weed,

hand
grubber

GREEN BEAN

until the vegetables
are ready for us
to pick

TOMATO

spading
fork

or dig up

carrot

potato

bushel basket

and carry home.
Then we wash them

onion

pail

and cut them and put them in a pot of water,

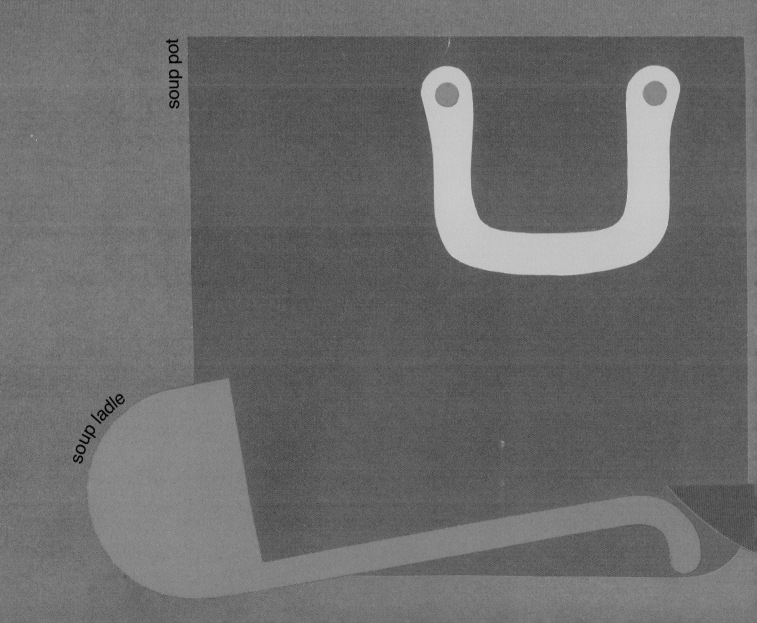

soup pot

soup ladle

carrot

corn

zucchini squash

tomato

onion

pea

broccoli

potato

pepper

green bean

knife

cabbage

and cook them into vegetable soup!

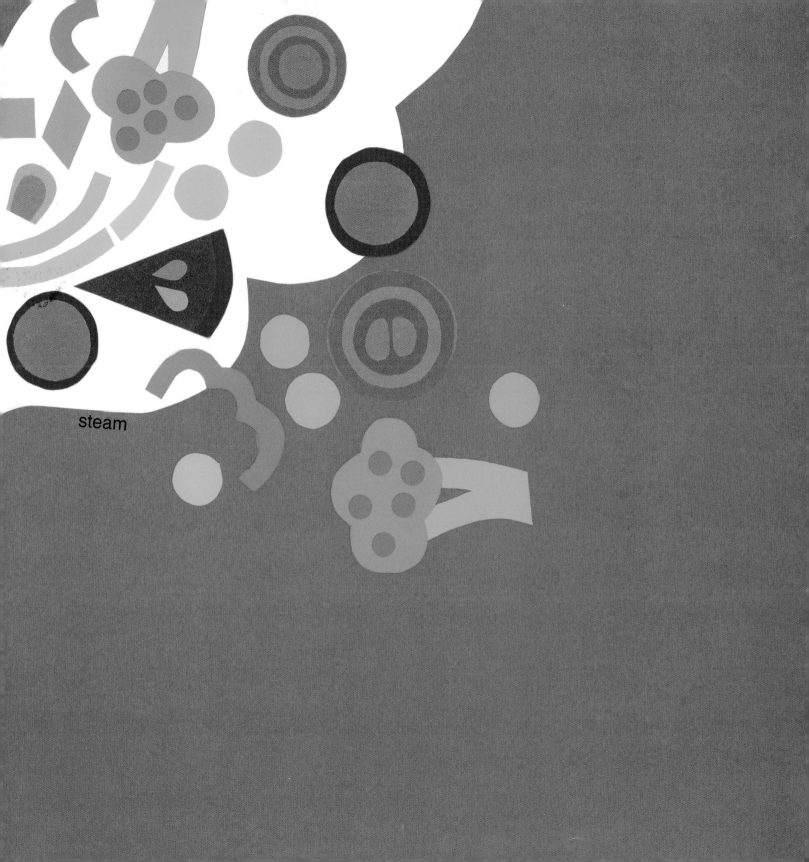

steam

soupspoon

soup bowl

At last it's time
to eat it all up!

It was the
best soup ever...

and we can
grow it again
next year.